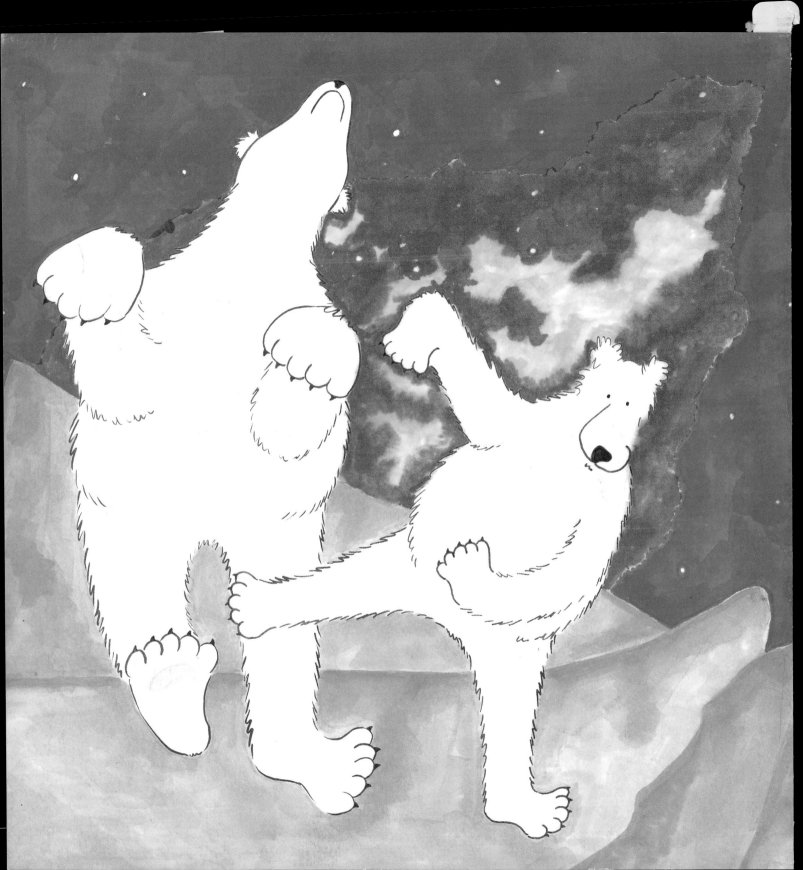

When I was a cub, I lived with my mother and my brother, Roy. We swam and we played and we ate little fishes. The Arctic night is long, and there are dancing lights in the sky. Sometimes, when the colored lights danced, we danced, too. We were polar bears, and that is what polar bears do.

Another thing polar bears do is travel long distances. I went a very long way and wound up in Bayonne, New Jersey.

I am the lifeguard at the swimming pool at the Hotel Larry. The hotel is named after me. I live there with Martin Frobisher, who owns the hotel; his wife, Semolina Frobisher; and their daughter, Mildred Frobisher.

My brother, Roy, also wound up in Bayonne, New Jersey. He has a job as a zoo bear at the Bayonne, New Jersey, zoo. I will tell you more about him later.

I often do little errands for Semolina and Martin Frobisher. For example, Martin Frobisher once asked me, "Larry, would you accompany little Mildred Frobisher when she goes to take her dancing lesson?"

"I would be happy to do so," I told Martin Frobisher. "Little Mildred Frobisher is a particular favorite of mine."

So twice a week after school, I walked with little Mildred Frobisher to Madame Swoboda's School of Dance.

As usual, when out in the street, I wore my long coat and big hat and sunglasses. This is necessary, because some people in Bayonne, New Jersey, are not used to seeing polar bears. Little Mildred Frobisher has been instructed to tell anyone who asks that I am her uncle from Milwaukee.

Usually, when little Mildred Frobisher was taking her dancing lesson, I would sit on the steps of the building and eat some fish sandwiches, which I carried in the pockets of my long coat. But one day I became curious and went inside to see what the dancing lesson was all about.

It was wonderful! Lots of little girls wearing special shoes were lined up, and Madame Swoboda, in a long dress, thumped on the floor with a long stick and told the children what to do. She would thump, thump, thump, and they would dance, dance, dance.

I found it very interesting.

Back in the Arctic, when I was a cub, one of us polar bears would just get up and dance—my mother or Roy or me. Then another bear would begin to dance, and soon we would all be dancing. That is how it is with polar bears.

So when Madame Swoboda was thumping, thumping, thumping and the little girls were dancing, dancing, dancing, it wasn't long before I needed to dance, too.

I took a place at the end of the line and danced with the children. It was very nice. I am a good dancer. All polar bears are good dancers. I thought it must be a treat for the children and Madame Swoboda to see a real polar bear dancing.

But Madame Swoboda said, "You! You are a polar bear! Stop! Stop at once!"

"Stop?" I asked Madame Swoboda.

"Stop," Madame Swoboda said. "You may not dance with the children."

"Why?" I asked. "Why may I not dance with the children?"

"Because this is a dancing class for children and not for bears," Madame Swoboda said.

"I think that is highly unfair," I said.

"All the same," Madame Swoboda said. "It is the rule."

On the way home, I asked little Mildred Frobisher, "Why would Madame Swoboda not allow me to dance with the children?"

"Madame Swoboda is strict," little Mildred Frobisher said. "She believes bears have no place in ballet."

"Ballet?" I asked. "What is ballet?"

"Usually ballet tells a story," little Mildred Frobisher said. "There is music. There are certain movements and positions of the feet. The dancers tell a story and express feelings through movement."

"Tell me more," I said. "Show me."

"Can you do this?"
"I can do that," I said.

"Can you do this?" little Mildred Frobisher asked.
"I can do that," I said.

"Oh, little Mildred Frobisher, I have a great desire to tell a story and express feelings through movement!"

The next day, I went to the zoo to see my brother, Roy. Roy is a good bear. The people who run the zoo trust him. He is allowed to come and go. Roy works with two other bears, Bear Number One and Bear Number Three. They are less good than Roy and me. They are allowed to leave the zoo only if Roy is with them.

"I have a great desire to tell a story and express feelings through movement!" I told Roy.

"So do I!" Roy said.

"I do, too!" said Bear Number One.

"I have a great desire to eat muffins," said Bear Number Three.
"And also to tell a story and express feelings through movement."
"But I cannot go to class with the children, because Madame
Swoboda believes bears have no place in ballet," I said.
"That is highly unfair," Roy said.

"Little Mildred Frobisher is a student of ballet,"
I said. "She has shown me the positions of the feet and
the movements of the arms."

"Show us!" said Roy and Bear Number One and
Bear Number Three.

"Can you do this?"   "We can do that!"   "Can you do this?"

"We can do that!"

"Can you do this?"
"Yes! We can do that!"

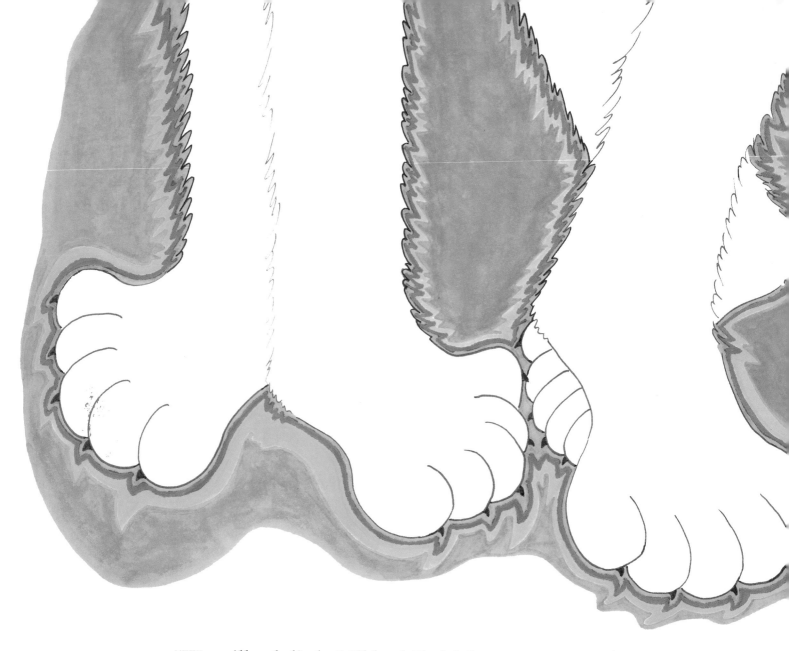

"We will ask little Mildred Frobisher to come to the zoo and teach us more," I said.

"We will practice," Roy said.

"We will learn to tell a story and express feelings through movement!" said Bear Number One and Bear Number Three.

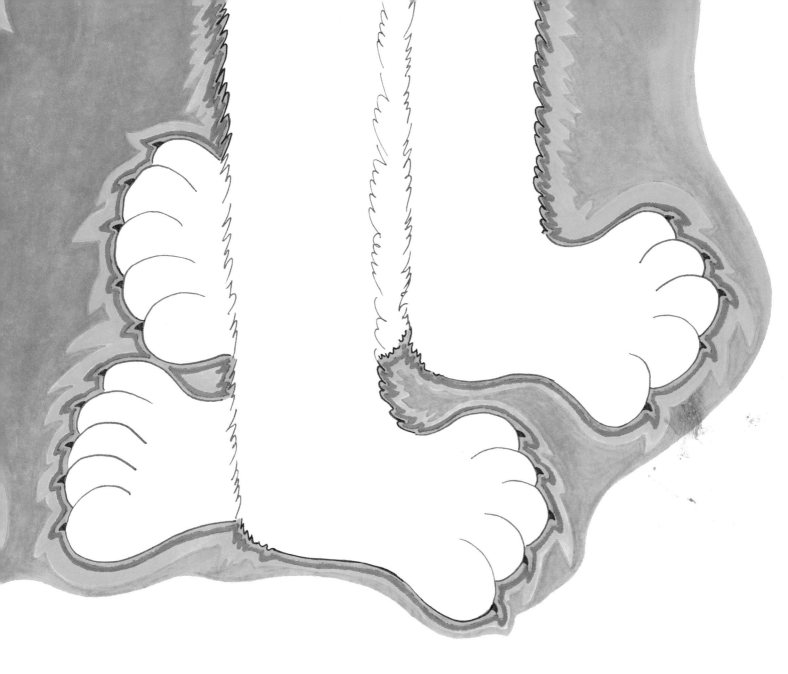

"There is more to my plan," I said.

"Tell us!" said Roy and Bear Number One and Bear
Number Three.

"I will tell you later," I said. "I will tell you in a few weeks."

A few weeks later, my friend Martin Frobisher
had beautiful cards printed:

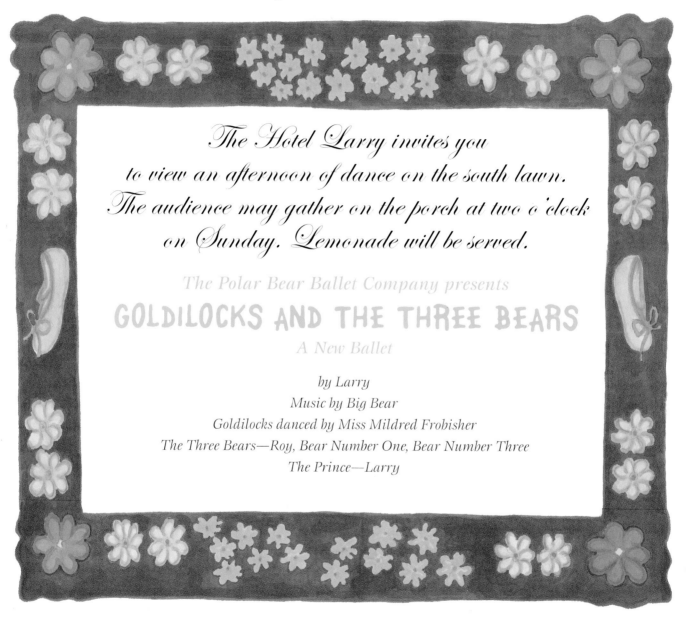

The Hotel Larry invites you
to view an afternoon of dance on the south lawn.
The audience may gather on the porch at two o'clock
on Sunday. Lemonade will be served.

The Polar Bear Ballet Company presents

GOLDILOCKS AND THE THREE BEARS

A New Ballet

by Larry
Music by Big Bear
Goldilocks danced by Miss Mildred Frobisher
The Three Bears—Roy, Bear Number One, Bear Number Three
The Prince—Larry

"I don't remember a prince in Goldilocks and the Three Bears," Roy said.

"There has to be a prince," I said. "I wrote one in."

"Will there be lots of people?" Bear Number One asked.

"We invited everyone—and Madame Swoboda," I said.

"Will there be muffins with the lemonade?" Bear Number Three asked.

"There will be muffins for the dancers after the performance," I said. "Blueberry."

Sunday was a beautiful day. Many people gathered on the big porch of the Hotel Larry. . . .

. . . Finis

To Meagan and Alex Julian,
who tell a story and express feelings through everything

Text copyright © 2006 by Daniel Pinkwater
Illustrations copyright © 2006 by Jill Pinkwater

Marshall Cavendish Corporation
99 White Plains Road, Tarrytown, NY 10591
www.marshallcavendish.us

Library of Congress Cataloging-in-Publication Data
Pinkwater, Daniel Manus, 1941–
Dancing Larry / by Daniel Pinkwater; illustrated by Jill Pinkwater.—1st ed. p. cm.
Summary: Larry the polar bear follows in the footsteps of little Mildred Frobisher's ballet class to
overcome strict Madame Swoboda's admonition that "bears have no place in ballet."
ISBN-13: 978-0-7614-5220-1
ISBN-10: 0-7614-5220-6
[1. Polar bear—Fiction. 2. Bears—Fiction. 3. Ballet—Fiction. 4. Dance—Fiction.
5. Humorous stories.] I. Pinkwater, Jill, ill. II. Title.
PZ7.P6335Dan 2006
[E]—dc22
2005001882

The text of this book is set in Esprit Book.
The illustrations are rendered in pen and ink and colored markers.
Book design by Adam Mietlowski

Printed in China
First edition
3 5 6 4 2

 Marshall Cavendish
Children